3 9082 07624 6241

W9-CBG-454

Laura & Mr. Edwards

THE LITTLE HOUSE CHAPTER BOOKS
Adapted from the Little House books by Laura Ingalls Wilder
Illustrated by Renée Graef

THE ADVENTURES OF LAURA & JACK
PIONEER SISTERS
ANIMAL ADVENTURES
SCHOOL DAYS
LAURA & NELLIE
FARMER BOY DAYS
LITTLE HOUSE FARM DAYS
HARD TIMES ON THE PRAIRIE
LITTLE HOUSE FRIENDS
CHRISTMAS STORIES
LAURA'S MA
LAURA'S PA
LITTLE HOUSE PARTIES
LAURA & MR. EDWARDS

Adapted from the Little House books by

LAURA INGALLS WILDER

illustrated by

RENÉE GRAEF

HarperCollins*Publishers*

Adaptation by Heather Henson.

Illustrations for this book are inspired by the work of Garth Williams with his permission, which we gratefully acknowledge.

Laura & Mr. Edwards

Printed in the United States of America. For information address HarperCollins Children's Books, a division of HarperCollins Publishers, 10 East 53rd Street, New York, NY 10022.
http://www.harperchildrens.com

Library of Congress Cataloging-in-Publication Data
Laura and Mr. Edwards : [adapted from the Little house books by Laura Ingalls Wilder] / illustrated by Renée Graef.
p. cm. — (A Little house chapter book)
Summary: When Laura and her family move from Wisconsin to Kansas, they make friends with a helpful neighbor who comes to their aid later when they settle in the Dakota Territory.
ISBN 0-06-027949-4 (lib. bdg.). — ISBN 0-06-442084-1 (pbk.)
1. Wilder, Laura Ingalls, 1867–1957—Juvenile fiction. [1. Wilder, Laura Ingalls, 1867–1957—Fiction. 2. Frontier and pioneer life—Fiction. 3. Neighbors—Fiction.] I. Wilder, Laura Ingalls, 1867–1957. II. Graef, Renée, ill. III. Series.
PZ7.L3723 1999 98-41708
[Fic]—dc21 CIP
AC

1 2 3 4 5 6 7 8 9 10
❖
First Edition, 1999

Contents

CHAPTER 1

A Log House

For as long as Laura could remember, she had lived in a little log house in the Big Woods of Wisconsin. But one spring, Pa decided it was time to move away. He wanted to go farther west and start a new little farm on the wide open Kansas prairie. So Laura and her big sister Mary helped Ma and Pa pack up a covered wagon with all their belongings. Laura's little sister Carrie was too small to help yet. She watched everything with big, round eyes.

For weeks Laura's family rolled along

in the covered wagon, traveling through woods and over rivers. When they finally reached Kansas, Laura saw that there were hardly any trees. There was only flat land covered with tall grass. The land stretched far into the distance. Overhead, the sky was big and blue.

Day after day, the little covered wagon drove through all that emptiness. There was no road to follow and there were no other covered wagons around. It seemed to Laura that they were the only people in the whole world.

One day, Pa brought the wagon to a stop.

"Here we are, Caroline!" he called to Ma. "Right here we'll build our house."

Laura and Mary scrambled down from the wagon in a hurry. All around them was the grassy prairie spreading to the edge of the sky.

To the north, Laura and Mary could just see a line of dark green treetops in the distance. That was a creek bed. On the prairie, trees could grow only beside a river or a creek.

Far away to the east, there was another line of green. Pa told them that that was the Verdigris River.

Right away, Pa and Ma began to unload the wagon. They took everything out and piled it on the ground. Pa took off the wagon cover and put it over the pile.

Then Pa got into the wagon. He drove right down into the prairie, out of sight.

"Where's Pa going?" Laura asked.

"He's going to get a load of logs from the creek bottoms," Ma answered.

For days, Pa hauled logs from the creek bed. He put the logs into two piles.

One pile was for a house, and one was for a stable.

When Pa had enough logs, he began to build the house.

First, he paced off the size of the house on the ground. Then he took his spade and dug two little hollows. Into the hollows he rolled two of the biggest logs. He made sure they were sound, strong logs because they would hold up the house. Pa said they were called sills.

Next, Pa took his ax and cut a wide, deep notch into each end of the sills. He took two more strong logs and cut notches into their ends. When the notches were cut, he rolled each log over so that the notches fit down over the notches in the sill.

Now there was an empty square on the ground, one log high. That was the foundation of the house.

The next day, Pa began to build up the walls. He notched each log before carefully rolling it up and fitting it snugly into the log below it. There were cracks in between the logs, but that did not matter, because Pa would chink those cracks.

All by himself, Pa built the house three logs high. Then Ma had to help him.

Pa lifted one end of a log onto the wall, and Ma held it in place while Pa lifted the other end. Then Pa stood up on the wall to cut the notches. Ma helped roll and hold the log while Pa settled it where it should be.

Every day, the walls were a little higher. Soon, Laura couldn't climb over them anymore.

One afternoon, Laura was tired of watching Pa and Ma build the house. She went into the tall grass to explore.

Suddenly she heard Pa shout, "Let go! Get out from under!"

The big, heavy log was sliding. Pa was trying to hold up his end of it, to keep it from falling on Ma, but he couldn't. It came crashing down.

Laura ran as fast as she could. Ma was huddled on the ground and Pa was kneeling down beside her.

"I'm all right," Ma gasped.

The log was on Ma's foot. Pa lifted the log and Ma pulled her foot out from under it.

Pa felt her to see if any bones were broken. "Move your arms," he said. "Is your back hurt? Can you turn your head?"

Ma moved her arms and turned her head.

"Thank goodness," Pa sighed. He helped Ma to sit up.

"I'm all right, Charles," Ma said again. "It's just my foot."

Quickly, Pa took off her shoe and stocking. He felt her foot all over, moving it gently.

"No bones broken," said Pa. "It's only a bad sprain."

"Well, a sprain's soon mended," Ma said in her cheerful voice.

Pa helped Ma to the tent. He built up the fire and heated water. When the water

was as hot as Ma could bear, she put her swollen foot into it.

Laura knew it was lucky that Ma's foot had not been crushed. A little hollow in the ground had saved it.

Pa kept pouring more hot water into the tub for Ma. Her foot was red from the heat. The puffed ankle began to turn purple. Ma took her foot out of the water and bound strips of rag tightly around and around the ankle.

"I can manage," she said.

She could not get her shoe on. So she tied more rags around her foot, and she hobbled on it. She got supper as usual, only a little more slowly. But Pa said she could not help build the house until her ankle was well.

The new log house must wait.

CHAPTER 2

A New Neighbor

One afternoon, Pa came whistling up the creek road. They had not expected him home from hunting so soon.

"Good news!" he shouted when he saw them all.

They had a neighbor. His name was Mr. Edwards, and he lived only two miles away on the other side of the creek. Pa had met him in the woods. Pa and Mr. Edwards were going to trade work, and that would make things easier for everyone.

"He's a bachelor," Pa told Ma. "He says he can get along without a house

better than you and the girls can. So he's going to help me first. Then as soon as he gets his logs ready, I'll go over and help him."

Now they would not have to wait any longer for the house. And Ma would not have to help build it.

"How do you like that, Caroline?" Pa asked joyfully.

"That's good, Charles," Ma said. "I'm glad."

Early the next morning, Mr. Edwards came walking across the prairie. He was lean and tall and brown. He bowed to Ma and called her "Ma'am," politely. But he told Laura that he was a wildcat from Tennessee.

He wore tall boots and a ragged sweater. On his head was a coonskin cap. He could spit tobacco juice farther than

Laura had ever imagined that anyone could spit tobacco juice. He could hit anything he spit at, too.

Laura tried and tried, but she could never spit so far or so well as Mr. Edwards could.

Mr. Edwards was a fast worker. In one day he and Pa built the walls as high as Pa wanted them. They joked and sang while they worked, and their axes made

the golden chips fly in the sunshine.

When they were finished with the walls, they set up a skeleton roof of slender poles. Then in the south wall, they cut a tall hole for a door. In the west wall and the east wall, they cut square holes for windows.

Laura couldn't wait to see the inside of the house. As soon as the holes were cut, she ran in.

Everything was striped. Stripes of sunshine came through the cracks in the wall. The stripes of sunshine were all across Laura's hands and her arms and her bare feet. Laura could see stripes of prairie through the cracks. The sweet smell of grass mixed with the sweet smell of cut wood.

Now the house was finished, all but the roof. Pa would build the roof by himself. In the meantime, they would drape the wagon cover over the rafters.

The walls were solid, and the house was large. It was a nice house. Laura couldn't wait to sleep inside it.

Mr. Edwards said he would go home now, but Pa and Ma said he must stay to supper. Ma cooked an especially good supper because they had company.

There was stewed jackrabbit with white-flour dumplings and plenty of gravy. There was a steaming-hot, thick cornbread flavored with bacon fat. There was molasses to eat on the cornbread. And Ma even brought out the little paper sack of pale-brown store sugar for Pa and Mr. Edwards to put in their coffee.

Mr. Edwards said he surely did appreciate that supper.

Then Pa brought out his fiddle. Mr. Edwards stretched out on the ground to listen.

First, Pa played for Laura and Mary. He played their favorite song, and he sang it. Laura liked that song best of all because on the last line, Pa's voice went down deep, deep, deeper.

"Oh, I am a Gypsy King!
I come and go as I please!
I pull my old nightcap down,
And take the world at my ease."

Then Pa's voice went deep, deep down, deeper than the very oldest bullfrog's.

"Oh,
I am
a
Gyp
sy
KING!"

They all laughed. Laura could hardly stop laughing.

"Oh, sing it again, Pa! Sing it again!" Laura cried.

Pa went on playing, and everything began to dance.

Mr. Edwards rose up on one elbow, then he sat up, then he jumped up, and he danced. He danced like a jumping-jack in the moonlight, while Pa's fiddle kept on rollicking, and his foot kept tapping the ground.

Laura's hands and Mary's hands were clapping together, and their feet were patting the ground, too.

"You're the fiddlin'est fool that ever I did see!" Mr. Edwards shouted to Pa with a wide grin. He didn't stop dancing and Pa didn't stop playing.

Baby Carrie couldn't sleep with all that music. She sat up in Ma's lap, looking at Mr. Edwards with round eyes, clapping

her little hands and laughing.

Even the firelight danced. All along the edges of the fire, the shadows were dancing, too. Only the new house that Pa and Mr. Edwards had built stood still and quiet in the moonlight.

After a while, Mr. Edwards said he must go. It was a long way back to his camp on the other side of the woods and the creek. He took his gun, and said good night to Laura and Mary and Ma. He said a bachelor got mighty lonesome, and he surely had enjoyed this evening of home life.

"Play, Ingalls," he called to Pa. "Play me down the road!"

So Pa played while Mr. Edwards went off down the creek road. Mr. Edwards sang in a loud voice as he walked. And Pa and Laura sang after him with all their might.

"Old Dan Tucker was a fine old man;
He washed his face in the frying-pan,
He combed his hair with a wagon wheel,
And died of the toothache in his heel."

Far over the prairie Pa's big voice and Laura's little one rang out. Faintly, from the creek bottoms they heard a last whoop from Mr. Edwards.

"Git out of the way for old Dan Tucker!
He's too late to get his supper!"

When Pa's fiddle finally stopped, they could not hear Mr. Edwards anymore. Only the wind rustled through the prairie grasses. The big, yellow moon was sailing high overhead, and the enormous sky was full of light.

CHAPTER 3

Mr. Edwards and Jack

When summer ended, it was time for Pa to make a trip into town. He needed supplies for the long winter ahead. The nearest town was forty miles away, so Pa would be gone four whole days. Laura knew the prairie would seem empty and lonely without him.

On the first day, Laura and Mary stayed in the house with Ma. Outdoors seemed too large to play in with Pa away. Laura noticed that Jack was uneasy, too, and watchful.

At noon, Laura went outside with Ma to help with the chores. They gave the colt water, and they moved the cow's picket-pin to fresh grass.

At milking time, Ma was putting on her bonnet again, when suddenly all Jack's hair stood up stiff on his neck and back. He rushed out of the house. They heard a yell and a scramble and a shout.

"Call off your dog! Call off your dog!"

It was Mr. Edwards! He was on top of the woodpile, and Jack was climbing up after him.

"He's got me treed," Mr. Edwards said, backing along the top of the woodpile.

Ma could hardly make Jack come away. Finally, he let Mr. Edwards come down from the woodpile, but he watched him every minute.

"I declare," Ma said, "he seems to

know that Mr. Ingalls isn't here."

Mr. Edwards said that dogs knew more than most folks gave them credit for. He told them that Pa had stopped by on his way into town and asked Mr. Edwards to check on Ma and the girls while he was away. Mr. Edwards was such a good neighbor, he had come at chore time to do the chores for Ma.

But Jack had made up his mind not to let anyone but Ma go near the cow or the colt while Pa was gone. Jack had to be shut in the house while Mr. Edwards did the chores.

When Mr. Edwards was leaving he said to Ma, "Keep that dog in the house tonight, and you'll be safe enough."

Soon the dark began to creep slowly around the house. The wind cried mournfully. The owls called, "Who-oo? Oo-oo."

A wolf howled, and Jack growled low in his throat. Mary and Laura sat close to Ma in the firelight. They knew they were safe in the house because Jack was there and Ma had pulled the latchstring. When the latchstring was pulled, no one could get inside.

The next day was as empty as the first. That evening, Mr. Edwards came to do the chores again. Once more, Jack treed him on the woodpile. Ma had to drag Jack off. She told Mr. Edwards she couldn't think what had got into that dog. Maybe it was the wind that upset him.

The wind had a strange, new howl in it. It sounded wild, and it went through Laura's clothes as if the clothes weren't there. Laura's teeth chattered while she helped carry wood into the house.

That night Laura listened to the wild

wind and thought of Pa. If nothing had delayed him, he would be in town now. And in the morning, he would be in the store, buying the things that they needed. Then, if he could get an early start, he could come partway home and camp on the prairie tomorrow night. And the next night he might be home.

The next day was very long. They could not expect Pa in the morning, but they were waiting till they could expect him. In the afternoon, they began to watch the creek road.

Jack was watching, too. He whined to go out. He walked all around the stable and the house. He stopped every once in a while to look toward the creek bottoms and show his teeth. The wind almost blew him off his feet.

When he came in, he would not lie

down. He walked about and worried. In a minute, he decided to go out. He went to see that the cow and calf and the colt were safe in the stable.

At chore time, Ma kept Jack in the house so he could not tree Mr. Edwards on the woodpile. Pa had not come home yet.

The wind blew Mr. Edwards in through the door. He was breathless, and stiff with cold. He warmed himself by the fire before he did the chores. And when he had done them, he sat down to warm himself again.

Mr. Edwards knew that Ma and Laura and Mary were worried that Pa had not come home. He said he could make himself right comfortable with hay in the stable. He would spend the night there if Ma said so.

Ma thanked him nicely, but said she would not put him to that trouble. They would be safe enough with Jack.

"I am expecting Mr. Ingalls any minute now," she told him.

So Mr. Edwards put on his coat and cap and muffler and mittens and picked up his gun. When he was all bundled up, he said good night.

Laura watched him walk away across the windy prairie. She missed Pa and wanted him home, but she felt safe with Mr. Edwards nearby. She knew they were lucky to have such a good neighbor.

CHAPTER 4

A Prairie Christmas

Pa soon came back from town with supplies to last them through the winter. He would not have to go to town again for a long time.

Now that winter had arrived on the Kansas prairie, the days were short and very cold. The wind howled and a hard rain fell. But there was no snow.

Laura and Mary stayed inside, close by the fire. They listened to the wind and the wet sound of rain as they sewed on their quilts and cut paper dolls from scraps of wrapping paper.

Every night was so cold Laura and Mary were sure there would be snow in the morning. But every morning when they looked outside the window, there was only sad, wet grass.

Laura and Mary were worried. There had always been snow at Christmastime in the Big Woods of Wisconsin. But here on the Kansas prairie, there was only rain. Laura was afraid that Santa Claus and his reindeer could not come without snow. Mary was afraid that even if it snowed, Santa Claus would not be able to find them. They were so very far away on the prairie.

When they asked Ma, she said that she didn't know.

"What day is it?" Laura and Mary asked her every day. "How many more days till Christmas?"

Laura and Mary counted the days on

their fingers until there was only one more day left.

Rain was still falling that morning. There was not one crack in the gray sky. They felt almost sure there would be no Christmas.

Still, Laura and Mary kept hoping.

Just before noon the light changed. The rain clouds broke and drifted apart. The sun came out and the birds sang. Drops of water sparkled on the grass.

Ma opened the door to let in the fresh, cold air, and they heard a loud roaring.

It was the creek!

Laura and Mary had forgotten about the creek. So much rain had made the creek wider and deeper. Now Laura and Mary knew they would have no Christmas. Santa Claus would not be able to cross that roaring creek.

Pa came in from hunting with a big fat turkey. He said it weighed nearly twenty pounds.

"How's that for a Christmas dinner?" he asked Laura. "Think you can manage one of those drumsticks?"

Laura said yes, but she didn't feel very happy.

Mary asked Pa about the creek. He said it was still rising.

Ma said it was too bad. She hated to think of Mr. Edwards eating his dinner all alone on Christmas day. Mr. Edwards had been asked to eat Christmas dinner with them.

Pa shook his head and said it would be too dangerous for Mr. Edwards to cross that creek now.

"That current's too strong," he said. "We'll just have to make up our minds

that Edwards won't be here tomorrow."

Of course that meant that Santa Claus could not come either.

Laura and Mary tried not to mind too much. They watched Ma get the wild turkey ready for Christmas dinner. It was a very fat turkey. Ma told them they were lucky little girls. They had a good house to live in, a warm fire to sit by, and a big turkey for their Christmas dinner.

Laura and Mary knew Ma was right. Still, they were not happy.

After supper they washed their hands and faces. They buttoned their nightgowns and tied their nightcap strings. They said their prayers quietly and went to bed.

Pa and Ma sat silent by the fire. After a while Ma asked Pa to play the fiddle.

"I don't seem to have the heart to, Caroline," he answered.

After a longer while, Ma stood up.

"I'm going to hang up your stockings, girls," she said. "Maybe something will happen."

Laura's heart jumped. But then she thought about the roaring creek and she knew nothing could happen.

Ma took one of Mary's clean stockings and one of Laura's. She hung them from

the fireplace. Laura and Mary watched her over the edge of their bedcovers.

"Now go to sleep," Ma said, kissing them both good night. "Morning will come quicker if you're asleep."

Laura closed her eyes. Even with the stockings hanging from the fireplace, it did not seem like Christmas at all.

CHAPTER 5

Mr. Edwards Meets Santa Claus

On Christmas morning, Laura opened her eyes. She heard Jack growl and then the door rattled.

"Ingalls! Ingalls!" someone said.

When Pa opened the door, Laura saw that it was still gray outside.

"Great fishhooks, Edwards!" Pa cried. "Come in!"

Laura looked toward the fireplace. The stockings were hanging limply.

Laura closed her eyes into the pillow.

She listened to Pa piling wood on the fire. She listened to Mr. Edwards tell how he had swum the creek with his clothes wrapped in a big bundle on top of his head. His teeth rattled while he talked and his voice shivered.

"It was too big a risk, Edwards," Pa said. "We're glad you're here, but that was too big a risk for a Christmas dinner."

"Your little ones had to have a Christmas," Mr. Edwards replied. "No creek could stop me after I fetched them their gifts from town."

Laura sat straight up in bed. "Did you see Santa Claus?" she shouted.

"I sure did," Mr. Edwards said.

"Where? When? What did he look like? Did he really give you something for us?" Mary and Laura cried at the same time.

"Wait, wait a minute!" Mr. Edwards laughed.

Ma said she would put the presents in the stockings, as Santa Claus intended. She said the girls mustn't look.

Mr. Edwards came and sat on the floor by their bed. He answered every question they asked him. Laura and Mary tried not to look at Ma, and they didn't see quite what was she was doing.

Mr. Edwards said that when he saw the creek rising, he knew that Santa Claus could not get across it.

"But you crossed it," Laura said.

"Yes," Mr. Edwards replied, "but Santa Claus is too old and fat. He couldn't make it, where a long, lean razorback like me could."

Mr. Edwards had figured that if Santa Claus couldn't cross the creek,

he would probably go into town.

So Mr. Edwards had walked the forty miles into town.

"In the rain?" Mary asked.

Mr. Edwards said that he had worn his rubber coat.

As soon as Mr. Edwards reached town, he saw Santa Claus walking down the street.

"In the daytime?" Laura asked. She didn't think anyone could see Santa Claus in the daytime.

"No," Mr. Edwards said. "It was night, but the lights from the stores shone across the streets."

Mr. Edwards told them that the first thing Santa Claus said was, "Hello, Edwards!"

"Did he know you?" Mary asked.

"How did you know he was really Santa Claus?" Laura asked.

Mr. Edwards said that Santa Claus knew everybody. And he knew Santa at once by his whiskers. Santa Claus had the longest, thickest, whitest set of whiskers west of the Mississippi.

So Santa Claus said, "Hello, Edwards! Last time I saw you, you were sleeping on a cornshuck bed in Tennessee."

And Mr. Edwards remembered well the little pair of red mittens that Santa Claus had left for him that time.

Then Santa Claus said, "I understand you're living now down along the Verdigris River. Have you ever met up, down yonder, with two little girls named Mary and Laura?"

"I surely do know them," Mr. Edwards replied.

"It rests heavy on my mind," said Santa Claus. "They are both such sweet,

pretty, good little things, and I know they are expecting me. I surely do hate to disappoint two good little girls like them. But with the water up the way it is, I can't ever make it across that creek. I can figure no way to get to their cabin this year.

"Edwards," Santa Claus continued. "Would you do me the favor to fetch them their gifts this one time?"

"I'll do that, and with pleasure," Mr. Edwards told him.

Then Santa Claus and Mr. Edwards stepped across the street to the hitching post where Santa's pack mule was tied.

"Didn't he have his reindeer?" Laura asked.

"You know he couldn't," Mary said. "There isn't any snow."

"Exactly," said Mr. Edwards. "Santa

Claus travels with a pack mule in the southwest."

Santa Claus opened the pack and looked through it. He took out the presents for Mary and Laura and gave them to Mr. Edwards.

"Oh, what are they?" Laura cried.

But Mary asked, "Then what did he do?"

Santa Claus shook hands with Mr.

Edwards and swung up on his fine bay horse. He tucked his long, white whiskers under his bandanna and said, "So long, Edwards."

Then Santa Claus rode away on the Fort Dodge trail, whistling and leading his pack mule behind him.

Laura and Mary were silent for a minute thinking of that.

Then Ma said, "You may look now, girls."

Laura saw that something was shining bright in the top of her stocking. She squealed and jumped out of bed. So did Mary, but Laura beat her to the fireplace.

The shining thing was a glittering new tin cup. Mary had one exactly like it. Now they had tin cups of their very own.

Laura jumped up and down and shouted and laughed. Mary stood still and

looked with shining eyes at her own tin cup.

They plunged their hands into the stockings again. Out came two long sticks of candy. It was peppermint candy, striped red and white.

They looked and looked at the beautiful candy. Laura licked her stick, just one lick. But Mary was not so greedy. She didn't take even one lick.

And the stockings weren't empty yet! Mary and Laura reached in and pulled out two small packages. Inside each package was a little heart-shaped cake. The tops of the little cakes were sprinkled with white sugar. The sparkling grains looked like tiny drifts of snow.

The cakes were too pretty to eat. Mary and Laura just looked at them. But at last Laura turned hers over. She nibbled a tiny nibble from underneath where it wouldn't

show. The inside of the little cake was white, too!

Laura and Mary didn't think to look in their stockings again. The cups and the candy and the cakes were almost too much. They were too happy to speak. But Ma asked if they were sure the stockings were empty.

Laura and Mary reached inside one more time. In the very toe of each stocking was a shining bright, new penny!

Now they each had a penny of their very own. A cup and a cake and a stick of candy *and* a penny! There never had been such a Christmas.

Laura and Mary were so happy they forgot about Mr. Edwards. They even forgot about Santa Claus.

In a minute, they would have remembered. But before they did, Ma asked gently, "Aren't you going to thank Mr. Edwards?"

"Oh, thank you, Mr. Edwards! Thank you!" Laura and Mary said. And they meant it with all their hearts.

Pa shook Mr. Edwards's hand, and then he shook it again. Pa and Ma and Mr. Edwards looked like they were almost going to cry.

"It's too much, Edwards," Pa said, shaking his head. They knew they could never thank him enough.

Mary and Laura looked at their cakes and played with their pennies and drank water out of their new tin cups. Little by little, they licked their sticks of candy, till each stick was sharp on one end.

Mr. Edwards had made it such a happy Christmas.

CHAPTER 6

Saying Good-bye

One morning, Mary and Laura were washing the dishes and Ma was making the beds. The cold winter was finally over. Now it was springtime, and Laura and Mary were talking about the garden. They couldn't wait to have vegetables again. All winter, they had eaten only bread and meat. Laura said that she liked peas best, and Mary said that she liked beans. Suddenly they heard Pa's voice outside.

Ma went quietly to the door. Laura and Mary peeped out on either side of her.

Pa was driving the horses from the field, dragging the plow behind them. Mr. Edwards was there, and so was Mr. Scott. Mr. Scott was their other neighbor. He lived in a house hidden in a little valley on the prairie. Now Mr. Scott was walking beside Pa, talking in a low voice.

"No, Scott!" Pa said to him. "I'll not stay here to be taken away by the soldiers like an outlaw! We're going now."

"What is the matter, Charles? Where are we going?" Ma asked.

Pa explained that they had to move off their land. When they had left the Big Woods of Wisconsin, the government in Washington had said it was all right to settle in Kansas. But now it turned out that Pa, Mr. Scott, and Mr. Edwards had settled on land that belonged to the Indians.

They would have to move right away. Mr. Scott had heard that the government was sending soldiers to take all the settlers out of Indian Territory.

Pa's face was red and his eyes were like fire. Laura had never seen Pa look like that. She pressed close against Ma and stood still, looking at Pa.

Mr. Scott started to speak, but Pa stopped him.

"Save your breath, Scott. It's no use to say another word. You can stay till the soldiers come if you want to. I'm going out now."

Mr. Edwards said he was going, too. He would not stay to be driven across the line.

"Ride along with us, Edwards," Pa said.

Mr. Edwards thanked Pa, but said that he didn't care to go north. He would make

a boat and go on down the river to some settlement farther south.

"Better come out with us," Pa urged him. "It's a risky trip, one man alone in a boat, going down the Verdigris."

But Mr. Edwards could not be persuaded. He said he had already seen Missouri. And he knew he could take care of himself on a boat.

Pa shook his head sadly. Then he told Mr. Scott to take the cow and calf.

"We can't take them with us," Pa explained. "You've been a good neighbor, Scott, and I'm sorry to leave you. But we're going out in the morning."

Laura heard all this, but she could not believe it. She did not really believe they were leaving their new farm and their beautiful new house until she saw Mr. Scott leading away the cow. The gentle

cow went meekly away with the rope around her long horns. The calf frisked and jumped behind. There went all the milk and butter.

Mr. Edwards told them that he would say good-bye, too. He would be too busy packing up to see them again.

First he shook hands with Pa.

"Good-bye, Ingalls, and good luck," he said.

Then he shook hands with Ma and said, "Good-bye, ma'am. I won't be seeing you all again, but I sure will never forget your kindness."

Then he turned to Mary and Laura. He shook their hands as if they were grown-up.

"Good-bye," he said.

"Good-bye," Mary said politely.

But Laura forgot to be polite.

"Oh, Mr. Edwards," she cried, "I wish you wouldn't go away! Oh, Mr. Edwards, thank you, thank you for going all the way to town to find Santa Claus for us."

Mr. Edwards's eyes shone very bright then. He smiled down at Laura and then he went away without saying another word. Laura watched him go.

She wished none of them had to leave the prairie. And she hoped she would see Mr. Edwards again someday.

CHAPTER 7

Mr. Edwards Helps Out

Laura and her family went back across the wide open prairie in their covered wagon. They rolled through Kansas and Missouri and Iowa to Minnesota, where Pa found them a little farm near a creek called Plum Creek.

Laura liked their new home, but farming was not always easy. After the first year, things did not go so well for Laura's family.

One winter, everyone except Pa and

Laura caught scarlet fever. The doctor came every day to tend to Ma and Mary and Carrie and the new baby, Grace. Pa did not know how he could pay the bill.

Worst of all, the fever had settled in Mary's eyes. Now Mary was blind. Her blue eyes were still beautiful. But she could no longer see out of them.

Pa knew it was time to move again. When spring came, he took a job with the new railroad out west. He sold everything to pay off the debts in Plum Creek, and the family moved to Dakota Territory.

Laura was excited to move farther west. She wondered what it would be like to live in a railroad camp.

The railroad camp was spread out beside a big lake called Silver Lake. There were shanties for the families and stables for the horses. There was a long,

low bunkhouse where the railroad workers slept. And there was the store where Pa worked. He was storekeeper for the railroad company.

"Caroline, we're among the very first out here!" Pa said when they were settled in their little shanty at the edge of the camp. "We've got the pick of the land for our homestead." They would live in the shanty until Pa found just the right piece of land for their new farm.

"That's wonderful, Charles," Ma answered.

When fall was over, the railroad workers began to move camp. The new railroad would keep moving farther west, but Pa said they would stay put. The land was good near Silver Lake, and he had found the perfect piece of land for their homestead. With the new railroad, Pa

said there would be more settlers soon.

Pa was right. Before winter was even over, people began arriving. The old railroad camp became a new little town on the prairie. The name of the town was De Smet.

With so many new people, Pa knew he had to file a claim on the land right away. Otherwise, someone else would take it. Pa had to travel a long way, to the town of Brookings, to file his claim. Early one morning, he set out.

Pa was gone a long time. Finally, after four days, he came smiling into the house.

"Well, Caroline! Girls!" he said, and his blue eyes sparkled. "We've got the claim."

"You got it!" Ma cried joyfully. She set the kettle on the stove for tea, and Pa sat down to warm himself.

"Did you have any trouble, Charles?" Ma asked.

"You wouldn't believe it," said Pa. "I never saw such a jam. It looks like the whole country's trying to file claims on land out here. When I showed up at the Land Office I couldn't get anywhere near the door. Every man had to stand in line and wait his turn. So many were ahead of me that my turn didn't come the first day."

"You didn't stand there all day, Pa?" Laura cried.

"Yep, Flutterbudget," Pa answered.

"Without anything to eat? Oh, no, Pa!" said Carrie.

"Pshaw, that didn't worry me," said Pa. "What worried me was the crowds. You never saw such crowds! But my worry then wasn't a patch to what came later."

"What, Pa?" Laura asked.

"Let a fellow get his breath, Flutter-budget!" Pa laughed, his eyes sparkling. "Well, when the Land Office closed I went along to get supper at the hotel, and I heard a couple of men talking. One had filed on a claim near Huron. The other said De Smet was going to be a better town than Huron, and then he mentioned the very piece of land I picked out for us. He was going to file a claim on it first thing next morning. He said it was the only piece of land left anywhere near this town-site. So he was going to claim it, though he'd never seen it.

"Well, that was enough for me. I had to beat him to that claim. At first I thought I'd be up bright and early next morning. But then I figured I wouldn't take any chances. So as soon as I got some supper I made tracks for the Land Office."

"I thought it was closed," said Carrie.

"It was," Pa answered. "I settled right down on the doorstep to spend the night."

"Surely you didn't need to do that, Charles?" said Ma, handing him a cup of tea.

"Need to do that?" Pa repeated. "I wasn't the only man who had that idea! Lucky I got there first. Must have been forty men waiting there all night. And right next to me were those two fellows that I'd heard talking."

Pa blew on his tea to cool it.

"But they didn't know you wanted that piece of land, did they?" Laura asked.

"No," answered Pa, "till a fellow came along and sang out, 'Hello, Ingalls! So you weathered the winter on Silver Lake. Settling down at De Smet, huh?'"

"Oh, Pa!" Mary wailed.

LAND OFFICE

"Yes, the fat was in the fire then," said Pa. "I knew I wouldn't have a chance if I budged from that door. So I didn't. By sunup the crowd was doubled, and a couple hundred men must have been pushing and shoving against me before the Land Office opened. There wasn't any standing in line that day, I tell you! It was each fellow for himself."

Pa paused and looked around. "How about some more tea, Caroline?" he asked with a smile.

"Oh, Pa, *go on!*" Laura cried. "Please."

Pa laughed and continued his story.

"Just as the Land Office door opened, the Huron man crowded me back. 'Get in! I'll hold him!' he said to the other fellow. He wanted to fight. And I knew that if I fought him, the other man would get my homestead. But then, quick as a wink,

somebody landed like a ton of bricks on the Huron man. 'Go in, Ingalls!' he yelled. 'I'll fix 'im! Yow-ee-ee!'"

Pa let out a loud screech.

Ma gasped, "Mercy! Charles!"

"You'll never guess who it was," Pa cried.

"Mr. Edwards!" Laura shouted.

Pa was amazed. "How did you guess it, Laura?" he asked.

"He yelled like that back in Kansas. He's a wildcat from Tennessee," Laura remembered. "Oh, Pa, where is he? Did you bring him?"

"I couldn't get him to come home with me," said Pa. "I tried everything I could think of, but he's filed on a claim south of here and must stay with it to keep off claim jumpers. He told me to remember him to you, Caroline, and to Mary and

Laura. I'd never have got the claim if it hadn't been for him. Golly, that was a fight he started!"

"Was he hurt?" asked Mary anxiously.

"Not a scratch. He just started that fight. He got out of it as quick as I ducked inside and started filing my claim. But it was some time before the crowd quieted down. They—"

"All's well that ends well, Charles," Ma interrupted gently.

Laura was disappointed. She had wanted to hear more about Mr. Edwards and the big fight. But she was so happy that Pa had made his claim. And she was happy to hear of that old wildcat Mr. Edwards again.

CHAPTER 8

A Surprise Guest

When spring came, Laura's family moved to the new homestead. There was already a little claim shanty on the land, so Pa wouldn't have to build a new house right away. Laura helped plant the new garden with pumpkins, beans, and potatoes. Pa planted corn, and by the end of the first summer, there was a good hay crop.

But winter came early that year. Pa and Ma could hardly believe it when a blizzard hit in October. After that, Pa didn't want to take any chances. The shanty was

fine for the spring and summer, but it wasn't good for a hard winter. Pa decided they should live in town until the next spring.

De Smet was full of people now. Laura didn't want to go into town and live among strangers. But she knew they would be warm and cozy in the store Pa had built.

Pa's store building was one of the best in town. He rented it out during the rest of the year, but now they would live in it. The store stood by itself on one side of Main Street. It was tall and square with two windows on the first floor and one window on the second.

Another blizzard hit soon after they were settled. Pa heard that a train was stuck in the snow a few miles outside of town. The train was carrying coal and

other supplies that the settlers needed. So Pa and some men from town decided to help clear the tracks.

The men were going to take a handcar from the train station. The handcar ran along the tracks. The men would pump it by hand and shovel away the snow as they went. Pa said they would be back in a couple of days.

Laura watched Pa put on an extra pair of woolen socks. He wrapped his wide scarf around his neck and buttoned up his overcoat. He fastened his earmuffs and put on his warmest mittens. Then he set off with his shovel over his shoulder.

Laura and Carrie walked with Pa through town. They were on their way to school, but they stood and watched as Pa headed for the station. They could see the handcar standing on the tracks. Men were

climbing onto it as Pa came up.

"All ready, Ingalls! All aboard," the men called.

Pa hopped onto the car and called, "Let's go, boys!"

The men began to pump the handlebars. Down and up, down and up, the rows of men bent and straightened. It looked like they were taking turns bowing to one another. Slowly, the handcar's wheels began to turn. Then the wheels began to roll faster and faster on the tracks, heading out of town.

Laura and Carrie heard Pa begin to sing, and then the other men joined in:

"We'll roll the o-old chariot along,
We'll roll the o-old chariot along
We'll roll the o-old chariot along
And we won't drag on behind!"

Up and down, up and down, all the men moved with the song. The handcar grew smaller and smaller, and the voices grew fainter and fainter. Finally, Laura and Carrie walked on to school.

All the rest of that day, and all the next day, there was an emptiness in the house. They were all waiting for Pa to come home.

"Surely Pa will be home tomorrow," Ma said at supper.

It was almost noon the next day when the long, clear train whistle sounded over the snow-covered prairie. From the kitchen window Laura and Carrie saw the black smoke in the sky. The roaring train was running along the tracks, and it was full of singing, cheering men. Laura could hear their loud, jolly voices echo through town.

"Help me get the dinner on, Laura," Ma said. "Pa will be hungry."

Laura was putting the biscuits on the table when the front door opened.

"Look, Caroline!" Pa called. "See who's come home with me?"

Little Grace had been running toward Pa, but now she stopped and stared at the open door. She put her fingers in her mouth and backed into Ma's skirts.

Ma put her gently aside as she stepped to the doorway with the dish of mashed potatoes in her hand.

"Why, Mr. Edwards!" Ma said.

"I told you we'd see him again, after he saved our homestead for us," said Pa.

Ma set the potatoes on the table and turned to face Mr. Edwards.

"I have wanted so much to thank you for helping Mr. Ingalls file on his claim," she said.

Laura stood quietly, watching Mr. Edwards. She would have known him anywhere. He was the same tall, lean wildcat from Tennessee. The laughing lines in his leather-brown face were deeper. But his eyes were as bright and laughing as she remembered them.

"Oh, Mr. Edwards!" Laura cried out after Ma had finished thanking him.

Laura and Mary began to talk about all the wonderful things Mr. Edwards had done for them years ago.

"You brought our presents from Santa Claus," Mary said.

"You swam the creek," Laura added.

Mr. Edwards grinned and bowed low.

"Mrs. Ingalls and girls," he said politely. "I surely am glad to see you all again."

Mr. Edwards said he couldn't believe how much Laura and Mary had grown.

"Are these really the small little girls that I knew down on the Verdigris?" he asked. When he looked into Mary's eyes, he realized that she could not see him. His face was soft and his voice was gentle.

Mary and Laura answered that they were those same little girls, and that Carrie had been a baby then.

"Grace is our baby now," Ma said. But Grace would not go to meet Mr. Edwards. She would only stare at him and hang on to Ma's skirts.

"You're just in time, Mr. Edwards," Ma said. "I'll have dinner on the table in one minute."

"Sit right up, Edwards," Pa cried. "Don't be bashful! There's plenty of food."

Mr. Edwards admired the well-built, pleasant house. He heartily ate the good dinner. But he said he was going west with the train when it pulled out. Pa could not persuade him to stay longer.

"I'm aiming to go far west," he told them. "This here country, it's too settled up for me."

As soon as dinner was over, they heard the train whistle blow loud and long.

"There's the call," said Mr. Edwards.

"Change your mind and stay awhile, Edwards," Pa urged him. "You always brought us luck."

But Mr. Edwards was determined to go. He stood up and shook hands with them all. He gently shook Mary's hand last.

"Good-bye all!" he called and walked quickly out the door. When he was on the street, they saw him run toward the depot.

Grace had watched Mr. Edwards the whole time wide-eyed and silent. Now that he had vanished so suddenly, she took a deep breath and asked, "Mary, was that the man who saw Santa Claus?"

"Yes," Mary said. "That was the man who walked forty miles in the rain and saw Santa Claus in town and brought back the Christmas presents for Laura and me when we were little girls."

"He has a heart of gold," said Ma.

"He brought us each a tin cup and a stick of candy," Laura remembered. She got up slowly and began to help Ma and Carrie clear the table. Pa went to his big chair by the stove.

Mary lifted her handkerchief from her lap. As she started to leave the table, something fluttered to the floor.

"Mary!" Laura cried. "A twenty-dollar—you dropped a *twenty-dollar bill*!"

Ma stooped to pick it up. She stood holding it, speechless.

"I couldn't!" Mary whispered.

"That Edwards," said Pa with a shake of his head.

"We can't keep it," Ma gasped.

But just then, they heard the last train whistle, clear and long, calling out good-bye.

"What will you do with it, then?" Pa asked. "Edwards is gone and we likely won't see him again for years, if ever. He's headed to Oregon."

"But, Charles," Ma softly cried. "Why did he do it?"

"He gave it to Mary," answered Pa. "Let Mary keep it. It will help her go to college."

Ma looked at the twenty-dollar bill in her hand. Last winter, she had heard that there was a college for the blind in Iowa. Ma and Pa were trying to save enough money to send Mary there. Pa must have mentioned it to Mr. Edwards.

"Very well," Ma said after a little while. Her eyes shone as she placed the bill in Mary's hand.

Mary held it carefully. She touched it with her fingertips, and her face glowed.

"Oh, I do thank Mr. Edwards," she said softly.

"I hope he never has need of it himself, wherever he goes," Ma added.

"Trust Edwards to look out for himself," Pa laughed.

Laura smiled to think of Mr. Edwards heading west, all the way to Oregon. She listened to the faraway rumble of the train as it rolled off across the fields of snow. Inside, she thanked Mr. Edwards, too.